P9-BAW-650

Two for the Road

ALSO BY RODDY DOYLE

Fiction

The Commitments
The Snapper
The Van
Paddy Clarke Ha Ha Ha
The Woman Who Walked Into Doors
A Star Called Henry
Oh, Play That Thing
Paula Spencer
The Deportees
The Dead Republic
Bullfighting
Two Pints
The Guts
Two More Pints
Smile
Charlie Savage

Non-Fiction

Rory & Ita

Plays

The Snapper
Brownbread
War
Guess Who's Coming For Dinner
The Woman Who Walked Into Doors
The Government Inspector (translation)
Two Pints

For Children

The Giggler Treatment
Rover Saves Christmas
The Meanwhile Adventures
Wilderness
Her Mother's Face
A Greyhound of a Girl
Brilliant
Rover and the Big Fat Baby

RODDY DOYLE

Two for the Road

VINTAGE

1 3 5 7 9 10 8 6 4 2

Vintage
20 Vauxhall Bridge Road,
London SW1V 2SA

Vintage is part of the Penguin Random House group of companies whose addresses can be found at global.penguinrandomhouse.com

First published in hardback by Vintage in 2019

penguin.co.uk/vintage

A CIP catalogue record for this book is available from the British Library

ISBN 9781529112269

Typeset in 10.5/13 pt Plantin MT Std
by Integra Software Services Pvt. Ltd, Pondicherry

Printed and bound in Great Britain by Clays Ltd, Elcograf S.p.A.

Penguin Random House is committed to a sustainable future for our business, our readers and our planet. This book is made from Forest Stewardship Council® certified paper.

12-7-14

— See the last o' the Ramones died.

— Gabba gabba sad, tha'.

— They were brilliant.

— Fuckin' brilliant.

— Did you ever see them?

— I did, yeah. A fair few times, actually.

— Good man.

— The best was the TV Club. D'you remember the TV Club?

— I do, yeah.

— The floor – d'you remember the floor? You could feel the music in it. Specially the reggae.

— Yeah.

— But the fuckin' Ramones, m'n – they nearly broke me fuckin' legs. The bass comin' up out o' the floor. I forgot abou' me eardrums.

— Must've been somethin', alrigh'.

— Ah, man. Incredible. I thought I was goin' to fall over. I had to grab the nearest arm to me.

— A woman.

— Exactly.

— Your Ma.

— Fuck off.

— Your missis.

— Nearly. Her brother.

— Hang on. You got off with your wife's brother?

— No – Jesus. Keep your fuckin' voice down. Yeh fuckin' eejit – where's your imagination?

— You said it was a woman.

— She was with him an' she grabbed his other arm at the same time. It was fuckin' gas.

— A scene from a shite fillum in the middle of a punk gig. The Ramones must be vomitin' in their graves.

— Well, that's only right an' proper.

— True.

31-7-14

— Gaza.

— The footballer?

— Don't even start now—

— Sorry – okay.

— The place.

— Dreadful.

— Shockin'. It's tiny, but – yeah? Gaza, like.

— Yeah, yeah – really small.

— An' Israel itself is only a small little country as well.

— I saw that on the news, yeah. I never realised it was so small.

— Smaller than Ireland, like.

— Way smaller.

— An' Gaza's only a tiny bit o' tha' space, yeah?

— Yeah.

— So there can't be all tha' many people livin' there, can there?

— No – I suppose not.

— So. Are they going to keep bombardin' it till there's no one left?

— It's lookin' like tha', isn't it?

— It fuckin' is.

— It's desperate.

— Kids.

— Yeah.

— Fuckin' kids.

— Terrible.

— History doesn't matter here, or who fuckin' started wha'. Yeh can't kill children.

— Fuck the cause.

— Exactly. Fuck blame an' revenge an' reprisal an' fuckin' – whatever. Even security.

— Or freedom.
— Nothin' justifies killin' kids.
— I'm with yeh, bud.

12-8-14

— See Robin Williams killed himself.

— Hard to believe.

— Yeah.

— To accept, like.

— Yeah.

— *Mork an' Mindy*.

— Hated it.

— Me too. Fuckin' hated it.

— Nanu fuckin' nanu.

— A load o' shite.

— Of course, we didn't know he was a comedian.

— Not back then, no. There were no videos or internet.

— We'd no idea he was fuckin' brilliant.

— Then – d'yeh remember *Good Mornin' Vietnam*?

— GOOD MORN-*ING*—

— Shut up, fuck sake. You'll get us barred.

— VIET-NAAAM – ! Great fuckin' fillum.

— But it wouldn't've been great if he hadn't been in it.

— That's true.

— *Mrs Doubtfire*.

— Class.

— I ended up fancyin' him, a bit.

— Only in the fillum.

— 'Course – yeah. Only when he was a woman.

— He was in some great fillums an' a lot tha' weren't crap only because he was in them.

— The best but— Have yeh seen *Happy Feet*?

— Ah, Jesus. Lovelace.

— No – the other one. He played two different penguins.

— Ramon.

— 'Let me tell something to joo.'

— Brilliant.

— 'Let me tell something to joo.'

— You nearly have him.

— I watch it with the grandkids – Jaysis – once a week.

— All that happiness. But he didn't want to live annymore.

— 'Let me tell something to joo.'

25-8-14

— You're lookin' a bit pale.

— The fuckin' ice bucket challenge.

— Wha'?

— One o' the grandkids challenges me. Grand. So I go out the back an' wait for me drenchin'. But yeh know those freezer bags for ice cubes?

— Yeah—

— They drop six o' those – rock fuckin' solid, like – from an upstairs window. Right onto me fuckin' head. I'm out cold.

— Jaysis—

— They get me into the van, straight up to Beaumont. I wake up when they knock me head off the path outside o' the A&E. An' inside! It's the fuckin' Alamo. Full of ice bucket casualties. There's a cunt with his head stuck in a bucket. There's seventeen women who've had heart attacks. There's a kid who's allergic to water – the fuckin' state of him. There's a lad who's attempted suicide cos no one's challenged him an' he feels left ou'.

— Fuckin' hell.

— So, I'm sittin' there – groggy, like. An' this sham asks if he can go ahead o' me. He's after cuttin' four of his fingers off. He holds up a Spar bag – full o' fingers, like. I ask him did he do it for charity, he says No. So I tell him to fuck off.

12-9-14

— See Jaws died.

— Paisley?

— Him too.

— Sad abou' Jaws.

— What abou' Paisley?

— Don't know.

— Yeah.

— Hard to know how to feel.

— He fuckin' hated us.

— He mellowed a bit in the end, but.

— That's true. But we all do tha'. Your man over there comin' out of the jacks. I used to think he was a complete cunt but now he's only a bollix.

— Paisley, but. Granted now, he calmed down an' talked to the Shinners an' they got peace an' tha' up there. An' that's all great. But he went a bit fuckin' overboard, didn't he?

— Grinnin' an' laughin' with McGuinness. He became Mother fuckin' Teresa.

— Peace is overrated anyway, isn't it?

— Borin'.

— I'll tell yeh, but. I'm grateful to him for one thing. Remember when he said the Pope was the antichrist?

— I kind of agreed with him.

— No, yeh didn't. Anyway, I was watchin' it on the News with one o' the kids. An' he says, 'Da, is the Pope really tha' man's aunty?' An' I start to explain it to him, an' then I think, 'It's all a load o' bollix.' Religion. It was liberatin'. An' I've the Reverend Ian to thank for tha'.

19-9-14

— Wha' d'yeh think o' Scotland?

— He should play four at the back an' a holdin' midfielder.

— Wha'?

— That's just my opinion.

— I'm talkin' abou' Scotland.

— Yeah. Your man tha' trains the Under 14s.

— He's not called Scotland.

— Is he not?

— He's called English.

— That's righ'.

— Frankie English.

— What about him?

— Fuck him – I asked you about Scotland. Although why I bothered, I don't know.

— Well. I seen a picture. People delighted, cos they'd voted No. An' tha' looked a bit weird – unnatural, like. Bein' happy an' sayin' No at the same time. It must be a bit like tryin' to pat your head and rub your tummy at the same time – you know tha' thing the kids do.

— Yeah.

— But I'll tell yeh. It must've been brilliant. The whole referendum. A vote that actually meant somethin'. Fair fucks to them. We should have one of our own.

— We're always havin' referendums. Yeh can't fart without a fuckin' referendum.

— A real one, but.

— Wha'? Givin' ourselves back to Britain?

— Maybe, yeah. Or ISIS.

— The Muslems?

— Yeah, why not? A bit o' crack. The speeches – can you imagine? Fuckin' brilliant.

— The Shinners would be up for it. They're fuckin' Sunnis already.

29-9-14

— Is it quiet in your house?

— Jesus, man. It's like a morgue.

— Same in my place. I have to be careful about every little fuckin' thing.

— A pain in the hole.

— I even had to tell her the dinner was lovely – earlier, like.

— Wha' was it?

— Can't remember. But it was grand. So I wasn't lyin', but—

— Fuckin' Cooney.

— Clooney.

— Wha' the fuck was he doin'?

— What he's done – what he's after doin' – it's worse than fuckin' climate change, so it is.

— Wha'?

— The world needs at least one good lookin' bachelor that isn't actually gay. A man who's gettin' better lookin' as he gets older.

— You've given this some fuckin' thought, haven't yeh?

— Well, I'd nothin' else to do an' she was clutchin' the remote like it was Clooney's langer. So, yeah. The women need to know there's always someone else – a bit better, like – out there.

— And now there isn't.

— Exactly. Because tha' fuckin' eejit has gone an' upset the natural order o' things. Fuck knows what's goin' to happen now. War, famine—

— No ridn'.

— The end o' the fuckin' species.

— He's a thoughtless prick, isn't he?

— A bollix.

15-10-14

— I was talkin' to this sham in a jacks?

— A jacks.

— Pub jacks.

— Wha' pub?

— Never mind wha' pub. I'm washin' me hands an' I say, 'They'll soon be fuckin' chargin' us for this.' An' he says he works for Irish Water an' we've got it all wrong.

— Did you deck him?

— Just listen. Yeh know when you're runnin' the tap for a mug o' water an' yeh wait till it's grand an' cold. Well, they won't chargin' us for tha'. Just the water in the mug. An' the same with showers. They'll only start chargin' when yeh get in under the water.

— That's fair enough.

— I'm not finished. Yeh know when yeh use the jacks, one flush sometimes isn't enough?

— I do.

— Well, they won't be chargin' for the second flush – if you provide photographic evidence.

— A photograph of your shite?

— A jpeg – yeah. But it has to come from an independent source. That's why they need our PPS numbers.

— Why?

— To verify tha' the picture of the shite didn't come from anyone in the house.

— So we have to get one o' the neighbours to come in?

— That's it.

— Jesus.

3-11-14

— See Acker Bilk died.

— I'm still reelin' after Alvin Stardust an' Jack Bruce. I can't keep up.

— How come?

— Did yeh not notice I wasn't here?

— I thought you'd gone a bit quiet.

— I wasn't fuckin' here.

— Well, like – how come?

— Ebola.

— Wha'?!

— There was an outbreak in the house.

— Hang on— D'you live in fuckin' Liberia?

— Just listen.

— Go on.

— Halloween. All the gang are in the house. Great gas – brilliant costumes. Anyway. I take a swig from the granddaughter's Coke. Lovely kid – sixteen. An' she says – she's jokin', like – it'll be infected. I say it's Ebola – I'm jokin' as well. The younger ones love the word an' they run ou' the back, goin', 'Ebola, Ebola!' One o' the neighbours—

— Let me guess. Special Trevor.

— The dopey cunt phones the HSE. The Ebola team arrives.

— In their space suits?

— Half us are already in fuckin' space suits. It's Halloween. The missis is in her Lady GaGa dress—

— The one made out o' the rashers?

— The HSE lads decide she's got foot an' mouth. Pande-fuckin'-monium. We're in lockdown for four days. I'm only after escapin'.

— Why are yeh dressed like Barry White?

— I keep tellin' yeh. It was fuckin' Halloween.

13-11-14

— What's the difference between smilin' an' smirkin'?

— Wha'?

— The difference between smilin' an' smirkin'. It's a political issue.

— Why is it?

— Tell us first – what's the difference?

— Well – if yeh ask me—

— I just fuckin' did.

— Fuck off. I'd say, if yeh don't like the sham who's smilin', then he's smirkin'.

— Yeah, I'll go with tha'.

— Like, the wife said to me – last Sunday, 'What're yeh fuckin' smirkin' for?'

— Does she not like yeh?

— No, she does. She says she does. Now an' again. But she said it after she'd said tha' Nidge was goin' to kill Siobhan, in *Love/Hate,* like. An' I said, 'Don't forget abou' Patrick Ward', just before Patrick ran into the garden an' shot Nidge. An' Siobhan.

— You smiled an' she saw a smirk.

— Yeah. Why is it a political issue?

— Well. Mairía Cahill said Mary Lou McDonald smirked at her in the Dáil yesterday.

— Well, that's because Mairía Cahill wouldn't be tha' fond of Mary Lou. Seein' as Mary Lou denies quite a lot o' wha' Mairía Cahill is sayin'. The real question is – why was Mary Lou smilin' at her in the first place?

— Why?

— Guilt.

— Cos she knows Mairía Cahill is tellin' the truth.

— That's it.

19-11-14

— See they're goin' to pay us for usin' the water.

— Wha'?

— The Government. Announced it today. They've decided not to charge us for the water. It's all been a bit of a misunderstandin'. So, instead, they're givin' each house 160 euros if they agree to accept the water. An' a free face cloth.

— Yeh have it arseways.

— I know. But it feels a bit like tha', doesn't it? Bunch o' fuckin' schoolyard bullies, an' now they want to be our best friends.

— Smug pricks tellin' us we'll have to pay for the water tha' we've always fuckin' paid for.

— Tryin' to frighten people.

— It'd take more than a drop o' water to frighten me.

— I'm not so sure – I can fuckin' smell yeh from here.

— Fuck off, you. Fuckin' Noonan, an' his comment abou' leavin' the taps runnin' if we're not charged.

— Fuckin' eejit.

— They never explained it. Yeh know why?

— They didn't think they had to.

— Bang on. They always forget it's a democracy. But with the last crowd, at least it took about ten years before they forgot. This gang, though—

— They're fucked.

— They are.

— Who'll replace them?

— We're fucked.

— We are.

20-11-14

— See Jimmy Ruffin died.

— Ah, man – I'll tell yeh. Tha' one made me really sad.

— 'Wha' Becomes o' the Broken Hearted'. It's brilliant.

— No question. An' that's the thing. I had his greatest hits.

— The record?

— Vinyl – yeah. An' I decided to go up into the attic, to find it.

— Bit of a fuckin' adventure.

— Fuckin' stop. I had the grandkids with me. Did yeh ever go up a ladder with nine kids?

— Seven's my record.

— An' there's a four-year-old holdin' the ladder for yeh.

— Boy or girl?

— Does it matter?

— Yeah.

— Girl.

— Go on.

— The place isn't properly floored, yeh know. The kids goin' fuckin' mad in the dark. The dust an' fuckin' cobwebs. But I found it.

— Good man.

— An' the record player as well. One o' the old mono ones. I had it on me head. Back down the ladder – fuckin' hell.

— An' the little girl was still there?

— Yeah.

— See now.

— I had to change the plug – it was an ol' two-pronged. But then we got it goin'. The grandkids had never seen a record before. They were fuckin' mezmerized.

— Brilliant.

— First record they ever heard – 'Wha' Becomes o' the Broken Hearted'.

— Perfect.

— Isn't it?

23-12-14

— See Joe Cocker died.

— What a fuckin' voice.

— Ah, man— But the best thing about him – he taught me tha' Beatles were shite.

— Hang on – wha'?

— Me brother – he's three years older than me – he brought home *Sergeant Pepper's*. An' everyone in the house loved it. Me ma sang 'When I'm 64' and she always cried at 'She's Leavin' Home', and me sister said, 'Don't worry, Ma, I'll never run away like tha'.' But she did – to fuckin' London. She even met a cunt from the motor trade. But that's a different story. Anyway—

— What's this got to with Joe Cocker?

— I'm gettin' there – calm down. They all loved 'A Little Help from My Friends' – in the house, like. Even me granny – an' she hated fuckin' everythin'. An' I just thought somethin' wasn't right. But then he – me brother, like – he brings home Joe Cocker's version. The single.

— Brilliant.

— No question. An' me da shouts, five seconds in – 'Turn tha' shite down!' An' I knew it – in me heart. That's the way it should be. If the oul' lad reacts tha' way, it's good. If he hums along, it's shite.

13-1-15

— Were yeh ever up in Ikea, were yeh?

— Oh, for fuck sake.

— We got fuckin' lost up there.

— Same here. We went up for a desk for one o' the grandkids an' we ended up buyin' a fuckin' hammock an' three cocktail shakers. An' never found the fuckin' desks. Wha' about youse?

— We were lookin' for some Mohammed wallpaper.

— Wha'?

— Wallpaper with pictures of your man, Mohammed, on it.

— For fuck sake. Did yis find it?

— No, we didn't. It was the wife's idea. She was fuckin' outraged tha' the Charlie lads were shot just because o' those cartoons an' she said we should wallpaper one o' the rooms with Mohammed. As a mark o' solidarity, like.

— Come here, but. Does Ikea sell Mohammed wallpaper?

— No, but we just thought any sham with a beard would do us an' we'd just say it was your man.

— Any joy?

— No – none. We thought abou' paintin' beards on One Direction but it would've have been a bit obvious.

— So, wha' did yis do?

— We went for a different cartoon instead.

— Which?

— SpongeBob.

— Hold on – you're hangin' fuckin' SpongeBob wallpaper in solidarity with Charlie Hebdo?

— We are, yeah. Je suis SpongeBob.

17-3-15

— Wha' d'yeh think o' this 'out o' control' drinkin' campaign?

— Brilliant. An' abou' time.

— How d'yeh mean?

— Well, after all this bolloxology abou' binge drinkin' an' drinkin' sensibly. It's good tha' they're encouragin' us to go ou' an' get hammered.

— I like the ad.

— The drunk kid with the hurley waitin' to knock the head off her poor sick ma when she comes out o' the jacks? It's a fuckin' masterpiece.

— Every teenager's dream.

— Exactly. An' perfectly natural. So, yeah. It's a breath o' fresh air, the whole campaign. Get ou' o' your face an' fuck the consequences.

— No matter how young.

— It's part of our culture.

— The only part that's worth a fuck.

— And funded by Diageo.

— About time they gave somethin' back – all the money they've made off the people o' this country. And let's face it. The fuckin' government would never put money into somethin' as brilliant as this. Another pint?

— Can't – no. Sorry. I've to go an' collect the grandkids.

— Where are they all?

— Dollymount. They're diggin' worms to put into their tequila slammers.

— See now. Makes yeh proud to be Irish, doesn't it?

— It kind o' does.

10-4-15

— See Barry Manilow's after gettin' married.

— Seen that, yeah. To a fella.

— But, like – didn't he have a song called 'Mandy' years ago? A love song, like.

— I think so, yeah.

— Well, she must've wrecked his fuckin' head. Cos he's after marryin' a chap called Garry.

— Well, good luck to him.

— Definitely.

— An' it kind o' makes sense, doesn't it? Marryin' a man at that age.

— How d'yeh mean?

— Well, they can sit up in the bed with their Kindles an' chat abou' the football. Instead o' havin' to pretend to be listenin' to her goin' on about her health or the state we're leavin' the world in for our grandkids, an' all tha' shite.

— Yeah, yeah – I kind o' get yeh.

— It'd be relaxin'. Yeh know – after singin' 'Copaca'-fuckin'-'bana' for the last fifty fuckin' years. Where's he from, an' anyway?

— Barry?

— Is he Canadian, is he?

— Don't know. I always thought he was – like – from somewhere else altogether.

— I've a feelin' he's Polish an' they moved to Canada, or somewhere like tha'.

— Annyway, he's shite, wherever he's from.

— No question. But good luck to him.

— Absolutely.

— Barry an' Garry.

— That'll be a song – wait an' see.
— 'Decided to marry.'
— Told yeh.

15-4-15

— See Percy Sledge died.

— Seen tha'. 'When a Man Loves a Man'. What a song.

— An' Jimmy Ruffin dyin' there as well, a while back. It's like all the great songs are dyin'.

— I know what yeh mean. I met me missis durin' 'When a Man Loves a Woman'.

— Hang on – fuck off a minute. You say tha' nearly every time a great singer dies.

— Well, she never remembered me.

— What is she – a fuckin' goldfish?

— Don't start – fuck off. I just didn't make much of an impression. It was me own fault.

— How come?

— Ah, I was just a bit overwhelmed. Terrified she'd say 'No' when I asked her up.

— An' did she?

— Say 'No'?

— Yeah.

— Every fuckin' time.

— But you kept at it.

— I did.

— And – don't tell me. She said Yeah durin' 'When a Man Loves a Man'.

— Yeah.

— How come?

— Well, she said later it was because of the song. She'd never heard it before an' she loved it an' she just wanted to dance with someone.

— That's kind o' nice.

— An' then she got sick on me an' she felt a bit guilty.

— An' she even fuckin' married yeh?

— Basically – yeah.

29-4-15

— Which way are yeh votin' in the gay thing?

— The marriage equality referendum?

— Yeah.

— Yes.

— You're votin' Yes?

— Yeah.

— Why?

— Me sister's son – me nephew.

— He's gay, is he?

— Yeah.

— So you're supportin' him.

— Have you become Joe fuckin' Duffy or somethin'?

— I'm just curious.

— Then, no, I'm not supportin' him.

— But you're votin' Yes?

— Look it, he's a grand kid but he's an irritatin' little prick as well.

— So— I don't get yeh.

— I'm watchin' the football, righ'. He always comes to the house when I'm watchin' the football. An' he sits beside me – grand. But then – say it's Real Madrid. He'll go, 'Oh, I love Ronaldo', or 'Pass it to Ronaldo.' So – like, last night, I lost it a bit and I said, 'What's so special about Ronaldo?' An' he says, 'His pace, his accuracy, his leap, his ability with the dead ball, the way he can turn, his engine – the stats speak for themselves.' Never mentioned his fuckin' hair or his six-pack or whatever they're callin' muscles these days.

— An' that annoyed yeh?

— Well, he fooled me. No – he made me think like a fool. An' he's always doin' it – catchin' me ou'. So, I thought to meself, 'A few years o' marriage will fix tha' little fucker's cough for him.'

— That's why you're votin' Yes? It can't be—

— No. I'm just messin'. Look – fuck it, I love him. He's a great kid an' if he ever wants to get married, he should be able to. An' me sister can have her big day as well.

— An' he obviously knows his football.

— Oh, he does, yeah.

— What's he think of James Rodriguez?

— Same as meself. Gorgeous an' over-rated.

6-5-15

— There was a ring on the bell there earlier.

— At home?

— Yeah – earlier. I was watchin' *Game o' Thrones,* so me head was full o' swords an' tits.

— We live in a golden age o' television drama.

— We fuckin' do. Anyway. There's a woman there – at the door, like – an' she's talkin'. But I'm still thinkin', like, 'I wouldn't mind bein' a dwarf.' So it's a while before I notice the 'No' sticker on her jacket – and her leaflets.

— Oh fuck – leaflets?

— She hands one to me an' she says, 'All children deserve their mother.'

— So I say, 'She's only gone to the shops – for smokes. She'll be back in a bit.' I'm wide awake now, so I say as well, 'While you're waitin', you could go across to number 78 an' tell the kids there tha' they deserve their mother. Cos she's in Mountjoy, playin' Monopoly with the Scissors Sisters.'

— Is she?

— No – she was cuttin' the fuckin' grass. But I'm on a roll now, so I say, 'An' what's marriage got to do with children? I've seven brilliant grandkids an' none o' their parents are married.'

— An' is tha' true?

— I'm not sure, to be honest with yeh – I can't remember. But I say, 'D'yeh have the Sky Boxsets at home?' She says she thinks so. So I tell her, 'Go on home an' watch a few episodes o' *Game o' Thrones*. An' when yeh see wha' the mothers get up to in tha' thing yeh won't be so quick with your leaflets. An' don't,' I tell her, 'don't write it off cos it's foreign. Cos it isn't. It was made in Ireland.' An' she says, 'I know it was. In Belfast. By Protestants.'

13-5-15

— Remember Barry Manilow got married there a while back?

— Can yeh imagine the music at tha' fuckin' weddin'?

— Jesus— But I was thinkin' about it again. Cos o' the referendum comin' up. That it's not a bad idea for men our age to get married.

— To each other, like?

— Yeah.

— Walk out on the missis—

— No, no – not necessarily. Just—

— If the circumstances were righ'.

— Kind o', yeah. It definitely makes sense. Doesn't it? Sharin' the gaff with someone like yourself. With the same interests.

— The football—

— Exactly. An' not havin' to pretend yeh care abou' all the woman stuff. Their health an' tha'. It'd be – I don't know – nice. Wouldn't it?

— An' that's another reason for votin' Yeah, d'yeh think?

— Yeah.

— Come here, but. What if the man yeh married turned out to be gay?

I never thought o' tha', mind you. So wha', but?

Wha'?

— Well – as long as he has the same interests. Football an' war— How many men are gay, an' anyway?

— Is it one in five?

— I think that's the fruit an' veg.

— That's righ'. It's one in ten – I think.

— One in somethin'. We'll say ten. So, there's only a one in ten chance tha' the man yeh marry would be gay. I could live with those odds.

— Come here. Say if your missis died or somethin'—

— Wha'?

— Hang on. An' say mine did as well. They were both in a car crash or somethin'.

— Who'd be drivin'?

— Yours.

— Go on.

— Well, like – would yeh marry me?

— No.

— Would yeh not?

— No.

— Hang on— Are you seein' someone else?

- - - -

— Are yeh?

- - - -

19-5-15

— One of me sons came ou' there earlier.

— Fuckin' hell. How d'you feel about tha'?

— Wha'?

— Your son, like. How did he come ou'?

— Through the back door. Same as the rest of us.

— Hang on. He came ou' the back?

— Yeah.

— You're fuckin' messin' with me again, aren't yeh?

— No, I'm not. Me son came ou' for a chat. We were ou' on the deck.

— Yis have a deck?

— Yeah.

— Since when?

— Since one o' the grandkids took a pallet from behind the Spar an' threw it on top o' the fuckin' grass. But – come here. Isn't it fuckin' amazin' tha' we can even have a chat like this?

— Abou' decks?

— No – abou' comin' ou' an' our kids an' stuff like tha'. Not so long ago—

— It would've been impossible.

— Well – not impossible. But—

— Fuckin' tricky.

— Very fuckin' tricky. But – more. There was a fella in my class in school an' – words like 'gay' an' 'camp' didn't exist back then the way they do now. But he got a terrible fuckin' time. From the the teachers an' the Brothers. Called him Twinkle-Toes an' stuff like tha'. They never let up – they battered him. An' we laughed. We had to – I remember thinkin' tha'. Or they'd've murdered us as well.

— Wha' was his real name?

— Jim. I was thinkin' about him there. Wonderin', yeh know, how he was. An' that's another reason I'll be votin' Yes.

— Why?

— Well—

— Apologisin'.

— Yeah – yeah. I suppose so.

— Same as meself, so.

24-5-15

— D'you read much?

— Wha'? Books?

— Yeah.

— Well, I do. I'd always read a few pages in the bed. War – I like books abou' war.

— Same as meself.

— Hitler an' tha'. I fall asleep every nigh' readin' abou' Hitler an' Stalin. Fuckin' gas, really.

— I read a bit of one last night. The wife is in a book club.

— Mine as well.

— What is a book club, exactly?

— Well, far as I can make ou'. Yeh go to a pal's house an' get fuckin' hammered. An' yeh bring a book with yeh, if yeh remember it.

— Grand. Yeah, I thought tha', meself. Anyway, she was readin' one – *The Bend for Home*. An' she keeps sighin' and laughin'. Getting' on me wick a bit. Cos I'm tryin' to read abou' the siege o' Stalingrad.

— I fuckin' love Stalingrad.

— Yeah – but, anyway. She goes ou' to the jacks an' I pick up the book. *The Bend for Home*, like. An' I read a bit – and, ah man – I'm tellin' yeh. It's brilliant – fuckin' brilliant now. The bit I read – abou' a Thursday afternoon – in the town he grew up in, like. It was amazin'. You were there when yeh read it.

— Sounds good. Who wrote it?

— Dermot Healy.

— Played for Sligo Rovers back in the day.

— Tha' was Keely. Healy – Dermot Healy. So anyway, she said she was finished it an' I got dug in. 'The doctor strolls into the bedroom and taps my mother's stomach.'

— That's the start?
— Yeah.
— An' yeh remember it?
— Yeah. There's a photograph of him on the back—
— Ah, hang on, for fuck sake. Just cos we voted for the same-sex thing, doesn't mean yeh have to fall in love with him.
— Ah fuck off. Anyway, look it, it's the business – the book.
— Sounds great alrigh'.
— Will I pass it on to yeh when I'm finished?
— Is Hitler in it?
— No.
— - - G'wan then – okay.

Dermot Healy: 1947–2014

25-5-15

— See Bill O'Herlihy died.

— I can't believe it.

— I know. Same here.

— I can't— He was brilliant.

— The best – him and the other lads. The best thing on telly.

— He was one o' those people— Did yeh ever meet him?

— No, but I know wha' yeh mean. It was like we knew him.

— An' liked him.

— Loved him.

— He took the football seriously.

— Like politics.

— Exactly. He took us seriously.

— He'd have the lads riled up an' you'd flick across to ITV an' there'd be ads, and yeh'd flick back to Bill an' the lads would still be shoutin' – an' yeh'd flick to BBC an' they'd be analysin' Thierry Henry's fuckin' cardigan. An' back to RTE an' Bill an' the lads would still be talkin' abou' football.

— No shite or fashion statements.

— Except Bill's tics.

— D'yeh know what it is? He made me happy.

— Yep.

— After watchin' him. I might be shoutin' at the telly. But I was always happy.

— You can't say more abou' the man, really, can yeh? He made us happy.

— Okey doke.

— Good night an' God bless.

28-7-15

— See one of the fellas that's runnin' for President of America says it's a good idea to bring guns into cinemas.

— He's bang-on there.

— Wha'?

— It'd make life a lot easier – listen. I went to the new *Mad Max* – me an' the missis. And about an hour in, you can tell Max is tryin' to say somethin'. To your one with her arm missin'. But, like, it's been a hard oul' day. An' seeing those young ones climbin' out o' the petrol tank, or wherever they were hidin' – you'd be hard-pressed to string a fuckin' sentence together after tha'.

— Weren't they gorgeous?

— Lovely. But annyway. Max – your man who plays him – is just about to talk when a cunt behind me starts shovin' popcorn into his fuckin' gob. An' I missed it. An' I think I should've had the right to turn around an' shoot the fuckin' eejit in the face.

— But—

— Not only tha'. I got done for speedin' on the way home.

— Hate tha'.

— Well, you try drivin' under fifty after seein' tha' fillum. An' not only fuckin' tha'.

— Wha'?

— I'd forgotten to take off the fuckin' 3D glasses, so I got done for reckless drivin' as well.

2-9-15

— See the Monkees are Unionists.

— Wha'?

— The Monkees. The group, like – off the telly, in the '60s.

— They're fuckin' Unionists?

— Yeah.

— One o' them's dead, but.

— The other one. The one with the woolly hat.

— Mike Nesbith.

— He's the leader of the Ulster Unionist Party.

— Wha'?!

— I heard it on the radio there a few days ago. Mike Nesbith, the leader of the UUP, said they were pullin' out o' the Northern Ireland Executive. Cos o' the IRA.

— What about the IRA?

— They're playin' *Game o' Thrones* again.

— The IRA doesn't exist.

— Neither does *Game o' Thrones* but we still watch it every night.

— It can't be the same Mike Nesbith. Was he wearin' the woolly cap?

— It was the fuckin' radio – I told yeh.

— Well, did he mention anny of their hits?

— What – like? Mike Nesbith, leader o' the UUP, said he thought love was only true in fairy tales an' for someone else but not for him.

— But then he saw her face.

— Now he's a believer.

— The IRA in *Game o' Thrones*. That'd be good.

— They're in it already. The fuckin' Wildlings.

7-9-15

— Didn't see you over the weekend.

— I was at the Electric Picnic.

— Fuck off. Were yeh?

— I went up on Friday. It's in – what's the county that no one comes from?

— Laois.

—Yeah. So I drove the granddaughter up. An' I'm gettin' her gear out o' the van and this girl doin' security must've thought I was as well, cos she throws one o' the yellow reflective jackets at me. An', like, I put it on and next of all I'm searchin' the bags. An' there's this lad has a plastic bag full o' yellow tablets an' he says they're for this asthma. An' I say, 'D'yeh think I came down in the last shower?', an' I take one.

— Oh, fuck. Wha' happened?

— I ended up playin' drums for Grace Jones. Don't fuckin' ask me how. But, by all accounts, I was very good.

— What's Grace like?

— Well, there now. The bass player – a nice chap – he tells me it isn't Grace at all. It's just a big bird puttin' on the Jamaican accent an' Grace is actually back in her hotel with a mug o' Horlicks. But then, I might've been dreamin' tha' bit. Or all of it.

8-9-15

— Yeh know these Syrians?

— Yeah.

— Well, I don't think they should be let into the country.

— Wha'?

— Until they can speak American.

— Fuckin' wha'?!

— Your woman from tha' top bit of America—

— Sarah Palin.

— Yeah. Well, she's dead righ'. An' Trump as well. You should listen to him. All these years the Spanish have been tellin' us they speak Spanish, an' they've actually been speakin' Mexican. The shifty fuckers.

— Hang on – wha'?

— An' the Portuguese have been speakin' Brazilian.

— Hang on – I need a fuckin' map.

— But the worst – no surprise, really. The English.

— They haven't been talkin' English.

— No.

— They've been talkin' American.

— Yeah. Accordin' to Sarah.

— The fuckin' bastards.

— Shakespeare me hole.

— Hang on, but. What do we talk then?

— Shite.

— The Irish talk shite?

— Fluent.

— So we'll only let in people tha' can talk shite?

— Yeah.

— Well, there'll be no fuckin' shortage of candidates.

— We have to be generous.

— And you know who'll be at the front o' the fuckin' queue?

— Who?

— Trump an' Palin.

20-9-15

— See Putin an' your man, the Italian with the painted head, drank a bottle o' wine tha' was two hundred an' forty years old.

— Fuckin' hell. Were they in the jacks tha' long?

— Wha'?

— They open the bottle, then one o' them has to go ou' to the jacks. At their age, like – it's understandable.

— What is?

— Goin' to the jacks.

— For two hundred an' forty fuckin' years?

— Well, you were in there a fair while, yourself.

— Fuck off.

— No, but. I suppose not. It would make more sense if they had to go two hundred an' forty times after they drank it. It must've been fuckin' rancid, but – tha' fuckin' old. Can yeh imagine skullin' a pint tha' was that old?

— Wine gets better with age.

— Yeah. But two hundred an' forty years? Who actually knows? It might've been nicer when it was two. But there's no one alive now who'd know. 'Cept Cher an' John Terry.

— Shows yeh what a pair o' cunts they are, but, doesn't it? Putin an' Berlusconi.

— Well, would you not like to be doin' it? Demolishin' somethin' priceless in a country you invaded, while the rest of the world falls apart?

22-9-15

— Righ'. Let's get this out o' the way. Did you ever ride a pig?

— Wha' part o' the pig?

— Head.

— No.

— Grand.

— What about yourself?

— No.

— No – same here. Nothin' tha' wasn't human.

— An' female.

— Probably, yeah. But—

— Wha'?

— No, it's nothin'—

— Go on.

— Well, I had this dog – when I was a kid, like. An' we were playin', on the floor in the kitchen. An' he stuck his tongue in me mouth an' I probably didn't shove him away as quickly as I should've.

— Ah, that's harmless enough.

— I was just relieved it wasn't a Christian Brother.

— Were yeh ever a member of a private club?

— Well, I have a SuperValu rewards card.

— Did yeh have to fuck a pig to get it?

— No. I filled in a leaflet.

— It's gas, but. Wha' the English Tories have to do just to prove tha' they can become fully fledged cunts. D'you think our lads do the same?

— Wha'? Like – stick it in a pig's mouth before you can join Fine Gael?

— It kind o' makes sense when yeh think about it. There's no other reason why yeh'd join Fine Gael. Is there?

2-10-15

— D'you ever go to plays?

— In a theatre, like?

— Yeah.

— No.

— Meself an' the missis went to one – a while back. She was on about us doin' somethin' a bit different. Instead o' the pictures. So, it's her birthday an' her sister got her two tickets for this play.

— An' did she expect yeh to go with her?

— I was fuckin' dreadin' it – all the fuckin' fuss, yeh know. But anyway, we go along.

— An' it was brilliant.

— How did yeh know?

— Your face.

— Well, it was. It was brilliant. *Faith Healer*, it was called. Your man, the Nazi, was in it.

— Ralph Fiennes.

— Him – yeah. He was very good.

— He's good in everythin'.

— That's true. But the play itself. Man – the words. There was him an' two others. An' they just talked – just fuckin' talked. But – brilliant. Spellbindin'. It was like listenin' to really interestin' people, except way better.

— Wha' made yeh think of it?

— Well, your man who wrote it died today. Brian Friel.

— I heard tha', yeah – on the news.

— So – yeah.

— It made a big impact on yeh. The play.

— It did, yeah.

— Have you been to any since?

— Plays?

— Yeah.

— No. Fuck tha'.

25-10-15

— See Maureen O'Hara died.

— The most beautiful woman that ever lived.

— I'm with yeh there, bud.

— She was a Dub as well.

— She was. A Southsider, but.

— Ah well, she had to have one flaw.

— I suppose so. But d'yeh know wha' was really amazin' about her?

— Wha'?

— She was so fuckin' funny.

— Gorgeous an' funny.

— It's some combination. She didn't even have to say annythin'. We've this thing – at home, like. We all watch *The Quiet Man* at Christmas, the whole gang of us. The grandkids as well – the little ones. An' I'll tell yeh, when Maureen O'Hara—

— Mary Kate Danaher.

— Mary Kate. The minute she walks onto the screen, the kids start burstin' their little shites laughin'. Before she even opens her mouth. And then when she does, there's no fuckin' stoppin' them. We all know tha' fillum off by heart.

— 'Who gave you leave to be kissin' me?'

— Brilliant. But my favourite is when she tells her brother, 'Wipe your feet.' The fuckin' head on him.

— An' when she wallops John Wayne.

— 'You'll get over it, I'm thinking.'

— Brilliant. The whole fuckin' thing. We'll have a pint for Maureen, will we?

— 'It's a bold one you are.'

14-11-15

— Paris.

— Fuckin' hell.

— Unbelievable. Can you imagine? Out on a Friday nigh'. An' that happens.

— Fuckin' savages.

— Fuckin' terrible.

— Were yeh ever there?

— Paris?

— Yeah.

— No, I wasn't – not really.

— What's tha' mean?

— Well, like – I was never in Paris but I'd nearly feel like I was, yeh know. Cos o' the – yeh know – the images an' the songs an' tha'. They're just so well known an' brilliant. The fillums an' stories – Pinocchio.

— Fuckin' Pinocchio?

— The Hunchback of Notre Dame.

— Tha' wasn't fuckin' Pinocchio.

— Who was it then?

— The other fella – I can't remember. Pinocchio was the little wooden fucker.

— That's righ'.

— Italian.

— That's righ'.

— Irritatin' little bollix.

— That's righ'. Anyway. Thinkin' about it – wha' happened last night, like. Football, music, a bit o' grub on a Friday nigh', a few drinks. They don't like life, the cunts tha' did it. Sure they don't?

— Looks tha' way, alrigh'. Quasimodo.

— Good man. That's the Hunchback.

— I remembered. I was worried there for a bit.

— 'The bells, the bells.' He was brilliant, Quasimodo, wasn't he?

— One o' the lads.

— Je suis Quasimodo.

7-12-15

— See someone from the RTE News got wet?

— I've never seen annythin' like it, never seen such fuckin' courage. She didn't even have her hood up.

— And did you see the cars goin' past her? She could've been splashed. But fair play, she stuck at it.

— I'll tell yeh – I remember seein' news reporters in Vietnam—

— Yeah, yeah. An' Biafra.

— An' Palestine.

— An' the tsunami.

— An' Belfast, don't forget.

— Yeah, yeah. An' there was tha' photographer on the beach on D-Day when the lads were landin'.

— All sorts o' fuckin' bombs an' whizz bangs goin' off all around him.

— It wasn't rainin' on fuckin' D-Day though, was it?

— He had it fuckin' easy.

— But your woman.

— She just stood there, in the wind an' the fuckin' rain.

— An' she told us that it was windy an' fuckin' rainin'.

— An' to stay in.

— A hero of our fuckin' times.

— 'Don't make unnecessary journeys.' She could've stayed in herself an' looked out the window.

— Exactly.

— But no. She put on her coat an' went ou'.

— Personality o' the Year.

— Future president, I'd say.

9-12-15

— See they're bannin' the munchies.

— The culchies?

— The munchies – they're bannin' the munchies.

— Wha'? Food?

— The Health Minister – fuckin' Varadkar. He's bannin' cheap alcohol. Says it causes obesity cos it encourages us to drink at home an' to eat too much, cos we get hungry when we drink.

— Well, he did his research – in fairness. He doesn't exactly look like he just escaped from Devil's Island, does he?

— Why doesn't he just fuck off an' mind his own business? Look after his own fridge.

— It's the nation's health he's worried about.

— Fuck the nation. I get this thing on Saturday nights. A *Match o' the Day* Special. A tray o' beer an' a pizza. A Polish chap delivers it – Stan. Twenty euro.

— That's not bad. What's the beer?

— It's one he imports, himself. Bally-Gdansk. It's not too bad. An' he texts ahead to see wha' pizza we want. We usually go for the Five Seasons.

— Five?

— Yeah.

— There's only four. Unless there's five in Poland, is there?

— No. Only the one, accordin' to Stan. The soggy bit in the middle – that's Poland. He throws it in as a bonus. He only charges for the four.

19-12-15

— Where were yeh? Haven't seen yeh in a few days.

— Ah—

— José?

— Yeah.

— It hit yeh.

— I'm fuckin' devastated.

— He lost the dressin' room.

— Fuck the dressin' room. He was brilliant. An' a bit fuckin' mad. An' tha' made him even better. But I'll tell yeh what it is. There are two men I should've been.

— Wha'?

— Your man, Quinn, from *Homeland*. He's the man I'd be if I didn't have kids an' responsibilities an' tha'. Quinn would go down to SuperValu the same way he goes about killin' Moslems. Yeh wouldn't see him tryin' to make his mind up between Brennan's an' Pat the Baker. There'd be bread all over the shop.

— Grand. An' Mourinho's the other man, is he?

— Yeah – absolutely.

— Why?

— He was enigmatic.

— Wha'?

— An' charmin'.

— Fuckin' wha'? You fancied him.

— No – yeah. No – fuck off. No. I just— My last birthday, I told the missis I wanted a José coat – yeh know?

— Yeah.

— But she's not really into the football and she got me Tony Pulis's tracksuit instead.

— It's not bad.

— Thanks.

— I'm not sure about the cap, though.

— Fuck off.
— In the pub, like.
— Fuck off.
— See Chelsea won yesterday.
— The cunts.

23-12-15

— Where would I find a drone?

— Your man over there beside the jacks. He's a fuckin' drone.

— The little flyin' yokes, I mean.

— The things the Yanks use for bombin' Afghanistan an' tha'?

— He's promised he won't bomb anywhere.

— Who?

— One o' the grandkids. Justin. A great kid. He wrote to fuckin' Santy.

— For a weapon of mass destruction?

— He said he'll only use it for deliverin' medicine an' food supplies.

— In the letter to Santy?

— Yeah.

— What age is he?

— Five.

— Fuckin' hell.

— He's a bright little lad. No spellin' mistakes either.

— As far as yeh know.

— Fuck off.

— Santy will be impressed.

— That's what I'm fuckin' worried abou'.

— Wha'?

— That young Justin will get the drone an' I'll spend Christmas in the cop-shop explainin' to the fuckin' Guards that he didn't mean to bomb Cabra or Syria, or fuckin' wherever.

— The drones the kids are gettin' – they're only little ones. Kind o' harmless.

— No fuckin' way.

— Wha'?

— No way is one of my grandchildren gettin' some cheap oul' thing – a fuckin' toy, like. It's military standard or nothin'.

— I'm with yeh there, bud. Only the best for the grandkids.

— An' fuck the consequences.

31-12-15

— Did yeh do well this year?

— Not too bad.

— Wha' did yeh get?

— Pyjamas, a stab vest an' a book about the S.S..

— A fuckin' stab vest?

— Yeah.

— Who gave you tha'?

— One o' the daughters. They were two-for-one in Aldi. One for me an' one for the missis. It's nice enough. Black – with 'Belgrade P.D.' on the front.

— Nice. Are yeh wearin' it now? Or are yeh after puttin' on a few kilos?

— No, I'm wearin' it. The daughter was in the house an' I wanted her to see me wearin' it, yeh know. Annyway, it's New Year's Eve. All sorts o' mad cunts in here you never see any other time o' the year. An' I'm goin' to the chipper on the way home. So—

— Better safe than sorry.

— Exactly. It's a bit fuckin' tight, but.

— A bit strange, but. Isn't it? As a present, like.

— I'm happy enough with it. Wha' about yourself? Wha' did you get?

— Some socks, a suicide belt an' a book abou' the Gestapo.

— Fuckin' hell – are yeh wearin' it?

— The socks?

— The fuckin' belt.

— I am, yeah. One o' the grandkids made it in home economics.

1-1-16

— I brought some o' the grandkids to the new *Star Wars* there earlier.

— Wha' was it like?

— A load o' shite.

— I heard it wasn't too bad.

— It was shite, I'm tellin' yeh. It looked like it was made in the Phoenix Park with a load o' wheelie bins painted white. Absolute fuckin' drivel. It made no fuckin' sense.

— Was Princess Leia in it?

— Yeah – played by Angela Merkel.

— That's alrigh', isn't it? Yeh'd trust Angela to save the world.

— Only if she's playin' Angela in a fillum about Angela. Not in this fuckin' thing. She looks lost. She couldn't handle a fart, let alone the European economy. But the worst bit—

— Go on.

— They're tryin' to find that irritatin' little prick from the first fillum. Luke Skypilot. An' d'you know where they find him? In all the fuckin' Galaxy an' infinity or wherever – where do they fuckin' find him?

— Where?

— Kerry.

— Fuckin' Kerry?

— Not even Kerry. A rock off the side o' Kerry. He's been hangin' off a stone in the middle o' the fuckin' Atlantic. Not a Spar or a pub in sight. An' this cunt is goin' to save us? For fuck sake.

11-1-16

— See David Bowie died.

— See now – tha' makes no fuckin' sense. Wha' you just said.

— I know wha' you mean. How can Bowie be dead? He was never alive, like the rest of us.

— Tha' makes no sense either. But it's bang on.

— I remember once, I was havin' me breakfast. An' I saw me da starin' at me. So, I said, 'Wha'?' An' he says, 'Are yeh goin' to work lookin' like tha'?' I was still servin' me time and, like, I was wearin' me work clothes. An' me overalls were in me bag. So I didn't know what he was on abou'. 'Get up an' look at yourself in the fuckin' mirror,' he says. I did, an' I was still wearin' me Aladdin Sane paint. Across me face, like.

— You were ou' the night before.

— Not really. Only down the road. Sittin' on the wall beside the chipper, with the lads. Sneerin' at the fuckin' world. But that was what it was like. Bowie was our God.

— He has a new record ou'. Last week, just. Know how I know?

— How?

— Me granddaughter. She showed me his video. 'Blackstar'. Unbelievable. Brillant. Scary.

— Business as usual.

— Exactly.

— It's so fuckin' sad.

— Yeah.

14-1-16

— See Bruce's pal died.

— Alan Rickman.

— Yeah. Hans Gruber.

— He was brilliant.

— Fuckin' brilliant. The best. 'I am going to count to three. There will not be a four.'

— He was great in everythin' – the *Harry Potter*s. Everythin'. The fuckin' head on him.

— Like, Bruce is the man – no question. But he's only as good, really, as the baddie in the fillum. An' Hans was the best.

— Ever. Up there with Lee Marvin.

— When I was watchin' *Die Hard* – the first time, like – I knew there'd be a sequel. I just knew, like. And – swear to God now – I was hopin' Hans would win so we'd see him again in the sequel.

— Instead o' Bruce?

— Yeah.

— You wanted Hans to trounce Bruce?

— Yeah.

— Wait now – hang on. I know wha' you mean – kind of. I think. But you wanted Bruce to die?

— Only for a bit – a fleetin' moment, like. Hans was just so fuckin' great. Like, I know it's blasphemy an' tha', sayin' that I wanted Bruce to get killed.

— Says a lot about Rickman, but – doesn't it?

— The same age as Bowie.

— Saw that.

— Frightenin'. Will we have another pint?

— 'What idiot put you in charge?'

22-1-16

— The man in black.

— I was at a funeral. A man up the road.

— I'm sick o' funerals.

— Same here. But this one – it was a bit different. He was from Mayo or somethin'– somewhere over there. So it was a real country funeral. The coffin in the house.

— With your man in it?

— Yeah, yeah. He was a big man now. Hands like shovels, yeh know. He looked great, but – in the coffin. Like he was just pretendin' to be dead an' he was listenin' to the chat. Squashed into it, he was. A huge man. Larger than life. Reminded me of my own da. A bit.

— They gave him a good send-off, so.

— Jesus, man. The funeral itself – in the church, like. Packed. Loads of his kids and grandkids. An' all sorts o' culchies up from Mayo. Tryin' their best to look like Dubliners, God love them. But packed now.

— I haven't been in a packed church since I was a kid.

— Yeah, yeah – same here. An' the speech at the end. One o' the sons. Christ, it was brilliant. But the best bit. When they were carryin' the coffin ou'. A lad with one o' those things yeh put on your shoulder—

— A bag o' cement.

— A violin. He played 'The West's Awake'. Made me proud, kind of – the whole thing.

— Proud o' wha'?

— Don't know. Just proud. An' sad.

— You're not goin' to start writin' poetry, are yeh?

— No, I'm not – fuck off.

3-2-16

— Wha' d'yeh think of the election?

— Well, two things went through me mind. 'Oh fuck, no,' and 'Abou' fuckin' time.'

— Same here. Except I only thought, 'Oh fuck, no.' But you're righ'. It's about time. They're fuckin' horrible.

— An' we're stuck with them.

— D'yeh think?

— Yeah. They'll win again – the Blueshirts.

— Not Labour, though.

— No – probably not. An' it serves them righ' for forgettin' they're Labour.

— It's the lies on the posters that I hate. The fuckin' slogans, yeh know.

— I saw one there earlier. 'Making Work Pay.' Fine Gael.

— They've been in power for five years and suddenly they want to end slavery. Cunts.

— But – it's weird. Yeh know what's worse? The posters with no slogans. Just a big fuckin' head. 'Vote for me.' But, like, I'm all in favour of democracy. Votin' an' tha'.

— Will we have another pint?

— Show o' hands.

— Two for, none against. There yeh go. Democracy in action. Now all we need is a fuckin' barman.

— Who would yeh like to win the election?

— Well – in an ideal world. A coalition of ISIS an' the Greens.

— Wha'?

— 'Turn off the lights or we'll fuckin' behead yeh.'

— Well, that's clear.

— An' honest.

23-2-16

— See Joey The Lips died.

— The wife told me. She was cryin' – an' two o' the grandkids. They loved him.

— Wha' was his name again – his real one?

— Johnny Murphy.

— That's righ'. He had a real Dublin head on him, didn't he?

— He was brilliant. 'I get snotty with no man.' Fuckin' brilliant.

— I seen him in a play once.

— Did yeh?

— Yeah. The wife was goin' with her sister but then the sister smashed her foot kickin' a bowlin' ball – don't fuckin' ask. So I went instead. I was fuckin' dreadin' it – I didn't even know he was in it. But there he was, an' he was brilliant. *Waitin' for Godot.*

— Was it any good?

— Great – yeah. Mad. An' Joey was amazin'.

— You know what's really upsettin'?

— Wha'?

— Well, he was the oul' lad in the fillum. But he was the only one tha' got off with the girls.

— He made us think there was hope for us all.

— An' now he's dead.

— I met him – I just remembered.

— When?

— Years back. I missed me bus – kind of on purpose. An' I went into the Flowin' Tide. He was in there.

— Wha' did yeh say?

— 'How's Imelda?'

— Wha' did he say?

— Nothin'. He just grinned.

27-2-16

— You're in early.

— Had to get out o' the house. I wanted to watch *Soccer Saturday* but the wife's watchin' the election count an' she owns the remote.

— She fuckin' owns it?

— A couple o' weeks back. I told her it was hers forever if she put the brown wheelie out, an' she refuses to accept that I was only jokin'. She carries it around in her fuckin' bag.

— Great day for the telly, all the same. The football an' the politics. I brought me tenner into Paddy Power's. There's me bettin' slip, look. Chelsea to beat Southampton, West Brom to draw with Palace an' Fine Gael to get four more seats than Fianna Fáil. Look at the odds.

— Yeh have Chelsea down to beat Fine Gael.

— Do I?

— Look.

— Fuck. I forgot me readin' glasses.

— They would as well – Chelsea.

— D'yeh think?

— Diego Costa against Leo Varadkar? Poor oul' Leo would end up on a trolley in one of his own A&Es.

— Fair enough. The election's all over the place. Any predictions?

— A coalition of Fine Gael, Social Democrats, Sinn Féin an' Leicester City.

23-3-16

— Fuckin' terrible week.

— Another one.

— Jesus, though – tha' family in Buncrana. Can you imagine?

— No. No – yeah. I can.

— Puttin' the brake on but the car keeps slidin' into the water.

— I know. Desperate.

— Tha' poor woman.

— I know.

— Her mother, husband, sister – an' the two little lads.

— The heart ripped out of her.

— An' Brussels.

— Fuckin' hell, man. Another o' those days where I was countin' my kids an' grandkids. Makin' sure they were all safe an' sound.

— I rang me daughter – the youngest.

— Where was she?

— The kitchen. But I didn't know tha' till I rang her. Just wanted to hear her voice, yeh know.

— Yeah. I don't know much abou' Brussels. Do you?

— No. An' even tha' makes me feel a bit shite. Like, are any o' the footballers from Brussels? Or the teams?

— They'd have to be. The place – the city, like – is huge.

— D'yeh know who's Belgian, but? The little red-headed fella.

— Prince Harry?

— Tintin.

— Is he?

— Yeah. An' Snowy.

— Oh, well then.
— He's only a cartoon, but.
— He's still one o' the lads.
— Je suis Tintin.

24-3-16

— Are yeh doin' anythin' for 1916?

— I was wonderin' about tha' on the way up. You know – would I have been in the GPO, or wherever, back then?

— And?

— At the age I am now, no – I don't think so. The toilet facilities are important. I'd want to know there's a decent jacks nearby before I'd start shootin' innocent women an' children.

— The GPO would have a good jacks.

— What abou' Boland's Mills, though? Or Stephen's Green. Behind a tree? No fuckin' way.

— It's the GPO or nothin'.

— Seriously, though – the way I am now, I'd be fuckin' terrified. Worried sick abou' the kids an' the grandkids, yeh know. Like in Brussels. Annythin' like tha', I'm lyin' awake, I'm checkin' on the kids, makin' sure the doors are locked.

— An' we'd've been bang in the middle of it, back then.

— Only around the corner, yeah. Forty kids died in 1916.

— I was readin' there. One of them died from a bullet tha' went right through her father first. A little young one on Moore Street.

— There yeh go. Fuckin' shatterin'. But then, I look at my kids – an' they're Irish. Rock-solid Irish. An' I like tha'.

— Me too – I know what you mean.

— An' that's what the Risin' was about – I think, anyway. The right to be different. The things tha' make us Irish. The little things.

— So, all the killin' an' the executions – they were for our right to say 'Thanks' to the driver when we're gettin' off the bus?

— That's half it, yeah.

— What's the other half?

— The right to call him a cunt when the bus is movin' off.

21-4-16

— See Prince died.

— It makes no fuckin' sense – at all. Is it definitely true?

— Yep.

— Me an' the missis—

— Don't tell me you met your missis when Prince was playin'. Yeh do that every—

— I wasn't goin' to – fuck off.

— Wha' then?

— Fuck off.

— No – go on.

— Well – when our oldest was born an' we were bringin' her home from the Rotunda. We hadn't a fuckin' clue. I mean, it was brilliant, havin' the baby. But we were fuckin' terrified. I was, anyway. We didn't even have a car seat. Or a fuckin' car, for tha' matter. We were in the van, the missis had her on her lap. Fuckin' madness.

— Tha' was normal back then, but. When was it?

— 1983. January. There was ice on the roads an' all. We were nearly afraid to talk, yeh know. An' I stuck on the radio.

— An' it's Prince.

— '1999'. Fuckin' perfect. We knew we'd be grand. It's a brilliant piece o' music, tha'. It became her song. We'd named her already but we started callin' her Princess an' – well—

— Are yeh alright?

— No – no, I'm not. I'll be grand in a minute. It's just shite, though, isn't it?

— Yeah.

23-5-16

— See we've a new barman.

— Where?

— Over there – over beside the till.

— Oh yeah. Hang on, but. He looks like— It isn't, is it?

— Louis Van Gaal – yeah, it is.

— Fuckin' hell. He got another job quick enough, didn't he?

— Yeah. Although—

— Wha'?

— Well, manager of the world's biggest football club to pullin' our pints. It's a big fuckin' career shift, isn't it?

— The money probably isn't as good either, is it?

— Wouldn't think so, no.

— He's pullin' a pint now, look it. God, he's fuckin' slow, isn't he?

— It's probably the job he should've been doin' all along.

— Wha'? Pullin' pints o' Guinness?

— There's the time, tradition, the whole routine. Orderin' a pint should be slow and very fuckin' predictable. Like Man United have been for the last few years.

— Look at him now.

— Wha'?

— Your man there just ordered a pint from him. An' look at Louis. He has his fuckin' clipboard out an' – what's he writin' in it?

— He's probably drawin' the pint. Plannin' how much of the glass he'll fill early doors.

— An' his route to the tap.

— I told yeh. It's the perfect job for him.

— Until the place fills up.

— Then he's fucked.

4-6-16

— 'I am the greatest.'

— He fuckin' was.

— He was— Well, he was Muhammad Ali. The name's enough, isn't it? Says it all.

— I was thinkin' there, rememberin'. He was fightin' an English lad – Brian London.

— I remember tha'.

— My da let me an' me brothers stay up to watch it. I can't remember exactly, but I think we might've gone to bed for a few hours an' he came in an' got us, an' the lights were off an' we went in to the telly an' it was off as well. An' remember back then, the telly had to warm up after you turned it on?

— I do, yeah. There'd be no picture for a minute.

— So, he went into the kitchen to put on the kettle an' he poured us cups o' milk and me ma had left a couple o' Clubmilks for us. So we gathered up the cups and went back in an' Brian London was on his back. The fight was fuckin' over.

— Brilliant.

— Me da was bullin'. For a minute, just. But I could see it on his face. This was better. The story, like. An' he told it all his life.

— And you were in it.

— I was.

— Tha' was nice.

— Yep.

25-8-16

— See Robbie Keane's retirin'.

— It's weird.

— Why?

— Well, like – he used to be a teenager.

— I think I know what yeh mean.

— I'll tell yeh – when you measure your life in football, it goes past very fuckin' quickly. One minute he's a kid, the next he's retirin'.

— He was great but, wasn't he?

— No question. Brilliant. An' the best thing about him – he had a real Dublin head on him.

— Yeah, yeah – I know what yeh mean. Richard Dunne, Duffer—

— Dublin heads.

— John Giles, Stapleton, Paul McGrath, Brady. You just see them an' you think—

— Dublin. They couldn't've been from anywhere else.

— But then yeh look at Roy Keane an' yeh think—

— Cork.

— Exactly. You might wish he was from Dublin but he wouldn't have been Roy if he'd come from anywhere else.

— You look at Shane Long an' yeh think—

— The sunny south-east.

— Shay Given?

— Donegal – no question. Seamus Coleman the same.

— Kevin Kilbane?

— Da from Mayo – his fuckin' ears.

— Robbie Brady?

— Northside.

— Stephen Ireland?

— Argos.

— D'you remember that goal Robbie – Robbie Keane, like – scored against Germany?

— Ah, man.

— Still makes me want to punch the air.

— Thank you, Robbie.

— Thank you very much.

29-8-16

— See Young Frankenstein died.

— Gene Wilder – yeah.

— Terrible, isn't it?

— Some o' those fillums he was in.

— Brilliant.

— Fuckin' brilliant.

— *The Producers*.

— 'I'm wet – an' I'm hysterical.'

— *Blazin' Saddles*.

— 'Little bastard shot me in the ass.'

— I met him once.

— Fuck off – where?

— Here.

— Fuckin' here?

— Dublin – yeah. When I was a kid. He was makin' a fillum. *Quackser Fortune Has a Cousin in the Bronx*.

— I'd forgotten tha' one.

— It wasn't his best. But annyway. They were filmin' on the street outside me house. Vans an' lights an' all – loads o' people. An' Gene Wilder was leanin' against the railings just down from me house. I didn't know who he was back then. An' I said to him, 'Are yis makin' a fillum, mister?'

— Wha' did he say?

— He smiled an' told me to say it again. He liked the way I said 'fillum'. It was better than 'movie', he said.

— That's nice.

— The first time I ever felt intelligent.

— An' the last.

— Fuck off.

— I told the grandkids there, when it was on the News. I told them Willie Wonka was dead. An' they were all cryin'.

— Says it all, really, doesn't it?

20-9-16

— See Angelina an' Brad have broken up.

— I couldn't give a shite.

— Ten years together, they were.

— I couldn't give a fuck.

— She wasn't happy with his parentin' style.

— I don't fuckin' care.

— Wha' does tha' mean – parentin' style?

— Don't know. His aftershave or his shirts or somethin'.

— I think there might be more to it than tha'. The whole package, I'd say.

— I'll tell yeh one thing, and it's the only thing I'll say on the matter. My missis has never complained abou' my parentin' style.

— Same here.

— Everythin' else, she's slaughtered me. But not tha'. Which makes me think.

— Wha'?

— She just doesn't like him. She's copped on – that's all. Brad's only a cunt, like the rest of us. He's human, like.

— So she might as well have married one of us.

— There yeh go. It's the good thing about gettin' old. See, the older he gets, the more he looks like us. An' the older we get—

— We look like Brad.

— Exactly. We all end up lookin' like Brad.

— Except Brad. What'll they do with the kids?

— Don't know.

— They've hundreds of them.

— They could give some o' them to Madonna, I suppose.

23-9-16

— You know *The Great British Bake-Off*?

— You're not still goin' on about 1916, are yeh? It's time to move on.

— The television programme. Have yeh seen it?

— I fuckin' hate cakes.

— Have you fuckin' seen it, I said?

— Yeah.

— An' it's a load o' shite, isn't it?

— It's the most popular thing on the telly.

— An' it's still a load o' shite. Fuckin' eejits makin' cakes. Who'd want to watch tha'?

— Millions o' people watch it.

— Fuckin' eejits watchin' fuckin' eejits makin' cakes. It was the main thing on the news. Just cos they're movin' to Channel 4.

— They're just worried – because it's Channel 4, like – tha' they'll make the contestants flash their tits or stir the cake mix with their langers.

— I just think it's fuckin' mad. An' today they're tellin' us tha' we're becomin' the fattest nation in the world.

— Fuck them.

— Who – the fat people?

— No – the fuckin' eejits who measure these things. The scientists an' tha'.

— At least we're good at somethin'.

— Wha'? Bein' fat?

— Well, it's a skill. It takes dedication.

— Some gobshite on the radio said fat should be a Leavin' Cert subject.

— Well, you'd get an A.

— Fuck off.

14-10-16

— See Bob Dylan won the Nobel Prize.

— Which one?

— Wha'?

— There's loads o' them. Bukes, science, accountancy – there's rakes o' the things. There's even one for fuckin' peace.

— Science then – I think.

— Fuckin' science? He won the Nobel Prize for science?

— Has to be, I'd say. That song, 'Mister Tambourine Man'.

— What about it?

— Well, how can one sham play a song with only a fuckin' tambourine? It can't be done. It's like givin' some poor fucker one o' them Irish yokes—

— A bodhrán.

— Exactly. An expectin' him to play 'Bohemian Rhapsody' on it. It's just not possible.

— But Dylan cracked it.

— That's me theory. But seriously—

— Go on.

— He deserves it. The buke – the literature – prize.

— I'm with yeh.

— I remember when me brother brought home *Highway 61 Revisited*, when it came ou', like. Now, I love me music – always did. But The Beatles, like – 'Love Me Do' an' tha'. I mean, there wasn't much in the lyrics of any o' the songs back then. An' then I heard Dylan singin' about the postcards an' the hangin' an' tha'. 'Desolation Row', yeh know. An' it was amazin'. The start of me life, nearly. Even me da stopped complainin' about the noise. For a minute.

9-11-16

— For fuck sake.

— Wha'?

— Did you ever think it would happen?

— Wha'?

— He'd get elected.

— Who?

— Trump.

— Who?

— Trump – Donald fuckin' Trump.

— What about him?

— Did yeh not see it?

— See wha'?

— The election – last night.

— What election?

— The American election – where were yeh? He's after gettin' elected.

— Who?

— Trump – I told yeh.

— Wha'?

— No, hang on – fuckin' hang on. How long are yeh goin' to keep goin' on like this?

— Four years.

— Ah, Jesus—

— Maybe eight.

10-11-16

— You know over in the States, the blue-collar workers tha' they say voted for Trump?

— What abou' them?

— Well, that's us, isn't it? We're blue-collar, aren't we? If we were over there.

— S'pose so.

— Even though your collar's a bit grey an' I've no collar at all. Unless a hoodie has a collar, does it?

— No, a hoodie has a hood. That's the fuckin' point.

— Thanks for the fashion tip, Melania.

— Fuck off.

— Annyway. We're blue-collar. Workin' class.

— So, you're wonderin' if we'd have voted for Trump if we were over there.

— Kind of.

— No fuckin' way.

— Are yeh sure, but?

— Yeah. I think so. Anyway, it's different here.

— How is it?

— Well, are you angry?

— No – sometimes, just. The water charges. Things like tha' – unfairness. But, like, the gays are grand and the women I know are brilliant an' I've no problem with the Africans. I'm a bit miserable but, generally, I'm grand.

— Maybe it's just America.

— That's wha' I was thinkin'. But then I heard abou' this letter that's been doin' the rounds in the HSE. Old people who take up hospital beds bein' referred to as 'trespassers'.

— An' your collar started to feel very blue.

— Yeah.

11-11-16

— See Trump killed Leonard Cohen.

— Saw tha'.

— He doesn't only hate women. He hates the men tha' women love. 'Specially older women.

— Fuckin' Clooney's gone into hidin'.

— Fuck him an' his Nespresso.

— And the Pope.

— Fuck the Pope?

— No. Women – they love him. Mine does, an' anyway.

— Poor oul' Leonard. He was good, but. Wasn't he?

— Ah, he was. You should hear me grandkids singin' 'Hallelujah'.

— Good, yeah?

— Fuckin' hilarious.

— The wife loved him.

— Leonard?

— She even became a Buddhist cos o' Leonard.

— Is tha' righ'?

— For a few weeks, just. Then she saw me eatin' a quarter pounder an' she said, 'Fuck the Eightfold Path.' But she's always on at me to wear a hat like Leonard Cohen's.

— Well, he won't be needin' it any more – in fairness.

— The thing is, but. If Leonard walked in here – if he wasn't dead, like – they'd all go, 'There's an interestin' man with a hat on him.' If I walked in, it'd be, 'Will yeh look at tha' fuckin' eejit with the hat.' An' that's the big difference between us an' Leonard Cohen. We couldn't even start bein' cool an' Leonard never even had to try.

24-12-16

— Will there be many in your place tomorrow?

— The whole gang, yeah. Can't remember how many exactly – it's into the hundreds.

— Jesus. How will yis manage?

— It's not too bad. We stick on *The Sound of Music* in two o' the rooms an' all the females an' two nephews bail in an' watch tha'. Then we assemble the cage.

— The cage?

— Yeah, yeah – Hell in a Cell. We started a few years back. All the men an' lads, four nieces an' a granddaughter.

— Yis fight?

— Yep.

— On Christmas Day?

— First thing – before the grub. We did it after the dinner once but it was a fuckin' killer – puke an' sprouts everywhere.

— Yis all get into a cage – where?

— The kitchen. Down to the kaks and covered in brandy butter.

— For fuck sake.

— It makes sense when you think about it. A year's worth of rage an' bitterness – get it out o' the system. Knock fuck out of one another, then it's good will to all men for the rest o' the day.

— What abou' the women?

— It's their turn after *The Sound o' Music*. An' I'll tell yeh, man – the hills are alive with the sound of envy.

28-12-16

— There's three generations o' women mournin' at home.

— Princess Leia?

— Yep.

— Same as my place.

— There's bit o' George Michael in the mix as well.

— Yeah.

— The *Star Wars* music an' 'Careless Whisper'.

— But mostly it's Carrie.

— Mostly Carrie – yeah. I mean, the daughters liked George, an' the wife – yeh know the way women, when they hit a certain age, they start to like gay men?

— No.

— No? Is it only in my house?

— Must be.

— Movin' on. Princess Leia.

— She was iconic.

— I don't know wha' tha' means, exactly, but you're bang on. I knew it after we got our first video. Back in the day, d'you remember?

— You had to throw turf into the back of ours.

— As big as a fuckin' cooker, ours was. Anyway, we got *Stars Wars* an' put it on. Our eldest daughter was only a little thing at the time an' she wasn't payin' tha' much attention. But then Princess Leia came on.

— An' she sat up.

— She fuckin' did. An' she's been sittin' up ever since.

— An' Carrie's mother's after dyin' as well.

— Fuckin' unbelievable.

— That's why they're stars, I suppose – is it? They're spectacular.

— George as well.

— Definitely – George as well.

27-1-17

— Was Hitler funny?

— Wha'?

— Before the war, like – say, 1937. Did people think Hitler was funny?

— Don't compare Trump to Hitler – please.

— I'm not.

— I'm fuckin' sick of it. Anything yeh say or do gets you called Hitler these days. At home, like. Even callin' the dog an eejit – I'm told I'm a fuckin' fascist.

— I know—

— And all dogs are eejits, by the way. It's a big part of the fuckin' job.

— I know – I'm with yeh. Hitler, but. Not Trump. Was he funny? Did people think he was just fuckin' ridiculous?

— Well, there was Charlie Chaplin.

— Yeah, yeah – *The Great Dictator.* Good fillum.

— Not tha' good.

— Okay. But they all went to it an' laughed an' came ou' thinkin', 'Well, that's Hitler nailed. What a silly little cunt.' An' then he went ahead an' did everythin' he did. It didn't matter if he was ridiculous. D'you get me point?

— Think so.

— So, Trump. I can't walk in the fuckin' door but there's a kid or a grandkid showin' me a funny Trump thing – on YouTube or whatever. But he's not fuckin' funny.

— No.

— An' the fuckers behind Trump – they're not funny either.

— No.

28-1-17

— See John Hurt died.

— Yeah, but did you see how many times he died?

— Wha'?

— One o' the kids showed me this thing on YouTube – 'The Many Deaths of John Hurt'. He started dyin' in 1962 an' he was still doin' it right up to the end.

— He was brilliant.

— Ah, man. I met the wife durin' *Alien*.

— Wha'?

— She grabbed me knee – when the yoke came out o' John Hurt's stomach. She nearly fuckin' knee-capped me and then her boyfriend wanted to box the head off me. So she gave him a box, decked the poor fucker. An' then we kind o' fell into each others arms.

— Yeh must've missed most o' the fillum.

— We went again the day after. She told me that when she felt my leg, she just knew I was the chap for her. An' the fact that I didn't object. She wanted to spend the rest of her life with me. So she said, an' anyway.

— When?

— An hour ago. When we heard it on the News.

— So John Hurt introduced yis, really.

— Yep.

— An' when did you get to feel her knee?

— Half an hour into *The Elephant Man*.

19-3-17

— See Chuck Berry died.

— I didn't know he was still alive.

— Same here. But he was. Till yesterday.

— It's a bit sad, tha'.

— It is. Kind o' forgotten abou'. Cos he was brilliant.

— Yeah.

— A brother o' mine – he was way older than me. He was out o' the house before I started school, nearly. Annyway, I used to love goin' to his flat. He was mad into Chuck Berry. An' the flat – it was like walkin' into America.

— Brilliant.

— Ah, man. There were road signs on the walls, for all the places in his songs. Memphis, Tennessee an' tha'. An' his wife – come here, listen. His wife – me brother's wife, like. She always called him her brown-eyed-handsome man.

— Were his eyes brown?

— One o' them, yeah. An' he called her Maybelline.

— An' her real name was—?

— Bernie. But they lived – the both o' them – inside Chuck Berry's music. An' I never met a happier couple.

— They still happy?

— They're dead – these years. Maybelline died a month after him.

— Heartbreak.

— She tripped over the record player.

29-3-17

— What abou' Brexit?

— Ah, fuck off – please.

— No – come on. Brexit.

— Can we talk abou' Trump instead? At least tha' cunt has a face.

— A chap on the radio this mornin' said it's the most important day since Dunkirk.

— Wha'?!

— So he said.

— Who?

— Didn't hear his name – an economist.

— The fuckin' eejit. Can yeh see the economists runnin' onto Omaha Beach, into enemy fire? Band o' brothers, me hole.

— Tha' was D-Day. He said Dunkirk. The retreat, like.

— Same thing – backwards. I'll tell yeh, but.

— Wha'?

— When yeh hear things like tha' – spoofers on the radio an' the telly. You can be sure o' one thing. They haven't a clue. An' when yeh hear Enda Kenny sayin' that Ireland will be negotiatin' from a position o' strength, you know for certain we'll be negotiatin' from a position in a galaxy far, far away. And when they use words like 'frictionless' an' 'seamless' to describe the new border, you can tell for a fact tha' the border will be a solid wall with razor wire an' cunts with rifles. It's goin' to be the worst kind o' nightmare.

— What's tha?

— A borin' one.

1-8-17

— Did you ever see *The Righ' Stuff*?

— Brilliant fillum.

— Your man from it died.

— Chuck Yeager.

— Sam Shepard – yeah.

— He was brilliant.

— I mean – I didn't know he was in so many things. But one o' the granddaughters is doin' a thing in college abou' fillums. Watchin' them, like.

— Can yeh do tha'?

— Yeah – she loves her fillums. A great young one, by the way. Anyway, she was in the house an' she tells us abou' this one. *The Assassination of Jesse James by the Coward Robert Ford*. I think that's the name of it, an' anyway.

— An' Sam Shepard's in it?

— Jesse's brother, yeah.

— Frank.

— Exactly. So we watched it.

— Good?

— Brilliant. Like, he was just brilliant in everythin', wasn't he? An' then she tells us abou' this one. *Paris, Texas*.

— Seen tha' one years ago. He's not in it, but.

— He wrote it.

— Fuckin' wrote it?

— Yeah.

— Jesus. He was married to Jessica Lange as well.

— There was no end to his fuckin' talents. So, we watched it.

— *Paris, Texas*?

— Brilliant again. They were bawlin' at the end. The wife an' the granddaughter.

— My wife says he was one o' the great handsome men.

— Same here.
— Bastard.
— Yeah.

9-8-17

— See Glen Campbell died.

— I was readin' a list of his songs this mornin'. Jesus.

— He was big in our house when I was a kid.

— Same here.

— Me father hated music – any o' the records me an' me brothers brought home.

— Same here, yeah.

— It was his job, like. I can see tha' now. A big part o' bein' a da.

— A pain in the arse back then, but.

— Every record we tried to play. 'Turn down tha' bloody noise!' Before we'd have the thing out of its fuckin' sleeve. It was fuckin' terrible. But then – one Saturday. One of us brings home 'Witchita Lineman'.

— What a song.

— Well, there yeh go. We put it on, and I look at me da, expectin' the roar. But his face—

— Transfixed.

— Fuckin' spellbound. He loved it. And then last nigh' – when we found ou' Glen Campbell was dead. We've one o' the grandkids stayin' with us – for a few nights, just. A lovely kid – she's sixteen. Anyway, she says, 'Who's Glen Campbell?' An' the wife tells her to look up 'Witchita Lineman' on YouTube.

— An' she was spellbound.

— She was, yeah. Exactly like me da.

12-11-17

— Come here – did you see that ad? The Marks an' Spencers one.

— With Paddin'ton Bear in it.

— That's the one.

— He's sound, Paddin'ton Bear. He's a nice, harmless fella. You could have a pint with Paddin'ton. An' that's more than yeh could say abou' most o' the others.

— What others?

— The fuckin' cartoons.

— I don't know. Bugs Bunny. You'd have a pint with Bugs, wouldn't yeh?

— Okay – yeah. He'd wear yeh out, but, wouldn't he? After a while. With all the fuckin' 'What's up, Doc', an' tha'.

— Good point – yeah. But the ad.

— What about it?

— You've seen it, yeah? Paddin'ton mistakes the burglar for Santy.

— It took me a while to cop on to tha'.

— Same here. But annyway. He brings the burglar back over the town, puttin' back all the presents tha' he's after robbin'.

— It's fuckin' gas, tha' bit.

— Well, it's mildly amusin'. But at the end, after the sham has seen the error of his ways. He leans down to Paddin'ton and he gives him a hug, an' he says, 'Fuck you, little bear.'

— I think it's, 'Thank you, little bear.'

— No, it's 'fuck you' – definitely. But why would he say tha'? To Paddin'ton, of all people.

— Well, he's after deprivin' the poor man of his livelihood – in fairness.

— Well, that's true.

1-3-18

— Fuckin' snow.

— The snow can fuck off with itself. I got home there at about four an' it was drifted up against the front door. I had to go round the back – had to climb over the gate. I haven't done annythin' like tha' since I was abou' ten – nearly broke me bollix.

— Hate tha'.

— Me hands were fuckin' numb. I could hardly hold the fuckin' key. An' then I couldn't get the door open.

— How come?

— Bread – there was a wall o' Brennan's bread up against the back door. The kitchen was full o' sliced pans.

— That's a bit fuckin' excessive – is it?

— Well, she – the wife, like – she was down in SuperValu an' she saw people grabbin' the bread and she doesn't know wha' came over her – some primitive urge or somethin'. She got into the ruck. She says she gouged some poor young lad's eyes ou' an' all he wanted was a cream slice. Anyway, she went back five times for more.

— For fuck sake.

— The best bit, but. She asks me what I want for me tea an' I say a toasted sandwich. Cos, like, we have the fuckin' bread. An' she says, 'No – fuck off – we're keepin' it for an emergency.'

4-4-18

— We're both a bit sad tonight.

— We are.

— Ray Wilkins.

— What a player.

— I'll tell you – Chelsea were never the same after he left. It's goin' back, I know. 1979, I think it was.

— You're righ'. That's when he came to United.

— If he wasn't dead I'd be callin' him a fuckin' traitor. Fuckin' United! But, anyway—

— He was brilliant.

— Brilliant – no question. One of the few brilliant things about Chelsea back then.

— A great passer o' the ball.

— His vision, man – Jesus. He knew where to put the ball two days before the fuckin' match. He was only eighteen when they made him the captain.

— That's the thing now – that's why it's so fuckin' sad.

— Wha'?

— His age. He was the first great player tha' was the same age as us.

— You're righ'. I remember, it was hard to accept at the time. I was askin' me ma if I could go out on Sunday night an' he was the captain of Chelsea.

— Here's somethin'. Ray Wilkins played against both George Best and Ryan Giggs.

— Is tha' true?

— It is, yeah.

— That's amazin'.

— Says a lot about the man, I think. A fuckin' giant.

27-4-18

— See Abba are back.

— Ah, that's sad.

— Wha' – why?

— Well, they were so – I don't know – iconic.

— Hang on – I didn't say they were dead.

— Oh.

— I said they're back.

— Oh – grand.

— Did yeh think they all died at the same time – all four o' them?

— Some sort o' suicide pact, yeah. They're Swedish. It wouldn't be tha' weird up there.

— In a fuckin' sauna.

— Listenin' to 'Dancin' Queen'.

— Well, I'd fuckin' kill meself if I had to listen to tha' shite too often.

— They've recorded some new songs.

— Ah, Jesus. I mean, they must be a fair age by now. Older than us, like.

— Yeah.

— Do you want to see a pair of oul' ones on zimmers singin' 'Take a Chance on Me'?

— It's a bit frightenin', alrigh'. But the new numbers might reflect their age.

— Here – 'Gimme gimme gimme Complan after midnigh'.'

— Good one. Annyway, I think it's kind o' nice.

— Tha' they've reformed?

— Yeah – it's nice.

— Is it?

— Ah, it is.

— They must've broken up – when? Must be nearly a hundred years ago, is it?

— Close enough, yeah. So, it's a good thing, is it?

— Ah, yeah.

— As long as we don't have to listen to them.

— Absolutely.

4-5-18

— Would you ever have an abortion?

— I only came in for a fuckin' pint.

— Would yeh?

— Look at me, for fuck sake. I'm not gettin' pregnant any time soon.

— Come on – the time has come. What's your opinion?

— Well – okay. Right— I've never told this to anyone outside o' the family.

— I'll tell no one.

— Doesn't matter. Years ago, one o' the daughters – she was sixteen. Just about.

— Pregnant.

— There yeh go. She hadn't a clue, God love her. An' the fella, he was sixteen as well. Clueless, the pair o' them. We asked her did she want it. She hardly knew wha' we meant. She just wasn't ready, like. So, anyway, the missis gets a number in London. She makes the appointment. Explains it to the daughter – is this what she wants? She says yeah, she thinks so. This is goin' back now – early '90s. So we book the flights – into town to book them. We half-expected to be arrested just for buyin' the tickets. Anyway, the wife goes over to England with her and I stay here. They were gone for three days.

— What was tha' like?

— Fuckin' dreadful. There were no mobiles or anythin'. I didn't know how it was goin' – how she was, like. Until the wife called. An' she was grand.

— Good – great.

— It was the secrecy I hated, but. Like we were ashamed. Cos we weren't – not really. It was like we were breakin' the law, an' I'm not even sure if we were. Just cos we loved our child.

— But it worked out okay, yeah?

— Yeah, but it was wrong. Smugglin' her out o' the country.

— You'll be votin' Yes, so.

— I'll be waitin' for the fuckin' doors to open.

14-5-18

— You know all the posters with the foetuses on them – the No ones?

— They're all over the fuckin' place.

— I seen a new one earlier.

— Another one?

— It says, 'I am only 9 weeks old. I can hack into your bank account.'

— Are yeh serious?

— It's outside Paddy Power's.

— Hang on – is it a Paddy Power's poster? One o' their ads?

— No – no. Calm down, for fuck sake.

— You're havin' me on, aren't yeh?

— I am, yeah. But yeh know the real one – 'I am 9 weeks old. I can yawn and kick'?

— Yeah.

— Well, yawnin'. It's not that impressive, is it? We can all do tha'.

— An' if he's yawning when he's nine weeks what's he going to be like when he's twenty-nine?

— Fuckin' unbearable.

— There yeh go.

— Come here, but. Your grandkids. Would yeh be worried abou' them seein' all them posters?

— Well, there now – I asked one o' me sons the same thing. He has two lads, like – two sons. An' he says not at all. They don't even notice the pictures. They're too busy countin' all the Yeses an' the No's.

— Brilliant.

— There's one o' the posters, but. The woman's body seems to be real but the foetus is definitely a drawin'. Have yeh seen tha' one?

— I have, yeah.

— Tha' one worries me.

— Why?

— Tha' poor young one – she needs to be warned. She'll be givin' birth to a cartoon.

— Barney Rubble.

— Exactly. Or SpongeBob.

16-5-18

— Does your missis ever drag you to plays?

— No. I mean – she made me go with her to the snooker in Goff's once, an' it wasn't too bad. An' a weddin' there recently. I can't remember who – it might've been one o' the kids. But not plays. Never.

— My one loves plays. An' she started gettin' me to go with her after she had tha' row with her sister.

— When was tha'?

— 1977.

— Jesus.

— They haven't spoken since. So, anyway, I've seen a fair few fuckin' plays in my time.

— There was a thing in the News this mornin'. Some playwright died.

— Tom Murphy.

— You've seen some o' his, have yeh?

— Loads o' them, yeah. There was one, but – in particular. *Bailegangaire*.

— Good?

— Ah, man.

— Wha' was it abou'?

— Women.

— Women?

— Women talkin'.

— It must've been fuckin' long, so.

— Don't start now – don't fuckin' start. There was a big bed in the middle o' the stage. With this oul' one in it. An' her two granddaughters comin' and goin' around her. It was amazin' – fuckin' mesmerisin'. An' I'll tell yeh, I've loved listenin' to women ever since. It was fuckin' brilliant.

— Come here – you're sad, aren't yeh?

— I am, yeah.

17-5-18

— Will yeh be watchin' the Royal weddin'?

— I will in me hole.

— Ah, come on – they seem like a nice enough couple.

— Me an' the missis, we're a nice enough couple. Will annyone be watchin' us?

— Well, like – first, yis aren't gettin' married, an' you're not a prince an' your wife, as far as I know now, isn't a fuckin' fillum star.

— It's a load o' shite.

— An' on top o' tha', yis aren't even a nice couple. You're a cranky pair o' cunts.

— At least we're interestin'.

— Fuckin' interestin'?

— Yeah – interestin'. The prince fella – what's his name? Harry. Name one single interestin' thing he's ever said or done. Go on, I'm right. Fuckin' nothin'. He's just like the rest o' them, a square-headed fuckin' dope.

— What about Meghan? She's been in fillums an' the telly.

— That's not interestin'. That's just actin'.

— Jesus, it's like sittin' beside fuckin' Death.

— Sit somewhere else then. Fuck off – go on.

— Here – listen. There's one really interestin' thing about Meghan.

— Wha'?

— Her ma.

— Her ma?

— Yep.

— - - - Wha' time is it on?

1-7-18

— Oh, Jesus – look over there.

— Where? Oh, fuckin' hell—

— Is that who I think it is?

— I think so.

— It's Lionel Messi.

— Yeah.

— An' that's—

— It's fuckin' Ronaldo. Sittin' there with him.

— What're they doin' in here?

— Well, they both got knocked out yesterday.

— So, they're on their fuckin' holidays?

— Yeah.

— In here?

— A bit of ordinary livin'. It has its attractions, I'd say – the pressure they're always under.

— In here, but. It's not exactly the Cliffs o' Moher.

— Messi's havin' a pint.

— I'd have expected tha'.

— An' what's tha' Ronaldo's drinkin'? It looks like gin – there's fuckin' cucumber floatin' in it.

— I'd have expected that as well.

— I felt sorry for them yesterday.

— A great World Cup, but, isn't it?

— Fuckin' sensational. Tha' kid, Mbappe.

— What a player.

— I've got grandkids that are older than him.

— It's funny tha', isn't it? How we age durin' the World Cup.

— Messi's gettin' up – look. He must be goin' to the jacks.

— He's headin' straight to the women's – look.

— Yeah – no. Jesus, what a swerve.

— Brilliant – amazin'. He had us all fooled. Fuckin' hell – did yeh see tha'?

— He got into the men's without openin' the door!

16-8-18

— See Aretha Franklin died.

— All those songs. Jesus, man, she was amazin'.

— Yeah, yeah. I met the missis when there was an Aretha song playin' – did I ever tell yeh?

— Hang on now – fuck off. Every time a singer dies you tell me you met your missis at one of their gigs or a dance.

— Well, I did.

— I'm not listenin'.

— You don't really know my wife. But I'll tell yeh. You're never goin' to woo a woman like tha' in one three-minute song.

— Woo?

— Yeah – fuckin' woo. It was never love at first sight, like. It was more like love at twenty-seven fuckin' sights. I had to win her over. An' that's where Aretha comes in.

— Okay – wha' happened?

— There was a club, a room over a pub, like – just off Capel Street. I can't remember wha' it was called. But they only played soul.

— Sounds good.

— It was. An' anyway, they're only playin' Aretha songs this nigh' an' I boogie up to the missis, an' I shout, 'R.E.S.P.E.C.T.'. Right in front of her, like.

— Wha' did she do?

— Well, there – she sang back.

— Wha'?

— 'F.U.C.K.O.F.F.'

— Tha' doesn't sound all tha' encouragin'.

— Ah, but – she was smilin'.

14-11-18

— It's sad about the Spider-Man fella, isn't it?

— Bruce Lee.

— Stan.

— That's him. Were you into Spider-Man an' all o' them when you were a kid?

— No.

— Same here. But my kids—

— Fuckin' mad abou' them.

— An' the grandkids. I hardly noticed the man had died until last night. One o' the daughters came over with her gang. An' they were all over me, tellin' me all abou' the different characters. It was like doin' the fuckin' Leavin' Cert.

— The *Spider-Man* fillums were great.

— Class. I liked his mott.

— Yeah.

— What was her name, the actor?

— Dunsten something. I had me own Spider-Man moment a few years back.

— Go on.

— In the son's house. The hall – they don't go for carpets. Bare floorboards, yeh know.

— Fuckin' eejits.

— I'm with yeh. But anyway, there's a Spider-Man mask on the floor an' I slip on it. The legs are gone an' I land right on me fuckin' back. An' the mask lands on me face. An' they're all there – the grandkids. They're lookin' at me an' the mask, then up at the ceilin'.

— They thought you were fuckin' Spider-Man.

— The happiest few seconds of my fuckin' life.

29-11-18

— Are you growin' a moustache?

— I am, yeah.

— At your age – for fuck sake.

— It's a disguise – fuck off.

— Disguise?

— Yeah.

— Why?

— I'm dead.

— Wha'?!

— I'm dead – officially.

— What's the story?

— Listen. One o' the granddaughters plays for the Under-11 girls. An' – don't ask me how – I've become their fuckin' manager.

— How come?

— Their regular coach eloped with a referee.

— Not Jimmy the Whistle?

— His brother. They've a whole family o' fuckin' referees. But anyway, she's a useful little player, the granddaughter. But our goalkeeper. Ah man, she's fabulous. She's six foot, three.

— What age is she?

— Ten. Hands like shovels. A lovely kid as well. But anyway, she couldn't make the match at the weekend. She had to go to a weddin'. An' the game was against the Arklow Amazons.

— They sound useful.

— Unbelieveable. They've a young one playin' for them tha' they're already callin' the Hacketstown Neymar. So, there's only one option. Get the game postponed. But the weddin' isn't a good enough excuse. We looked up the rules, like.

— A death.

— Exactly. So I phone the league an' I tell them the manager's after dyin'. But I forgot I was the fuckin' manager.

— For fuck sake—

— They're all comin' to the fuckin' funeral – all the heads from the FAI. Mick McCarthy an' all.

— When's the funeral?

— Tomorrow mornin'.

— Yeh fuckin' eejit.

— I know.

1-2-19

— D'you have your breakfast every mornin'?

— I do, yeah. Although it depends how you define 'mornin''.

— Wha' d'you mean?

— Well today, like, I had me breakfast last nigh' – if tha' makes sense. Before I went to bed. I just thought I'd get it out o' the way. But, yeah, I'd always have a good breakfast.

— The most important meal o' the day.

— Absolutely.

— It isn't.

— Wha'?

— The most important meal of the fuckin' day.

— Says who?

— The scientists – the fuckin' experts. Again.

— Tha' can't be righ'.

— So they're sayin', an' anyway. It was on the News earlier – before Brexit an' all.

— My Ma used to say it.

— Same here.

— Eat all o' it now. It's the most important—

— Meal o' the day. Same here, yeah.

— So. The scientists – they're sayin' my Ma was a liar.

— More or less.

— The woman who gave birth to me, mind. She was just havin' us on?

— That's wha' they're implyin'.

— I'd imply their bollixes if I met them. What is the most important meal then? If it isn't the breakfast.

— They didn't say.

— An' that's typical as well, isn't it? An' I'll tell yeh one thing. I bet it's not the dinner.

— That'd be too fuckin' obvious, wouldn't it?

14-3-19

— See Georgie Burgess died.

— Pat Laffin.

— That's him – Georgie.

— He was brilliant in *The Snapper*, wasn't he?

— Brilliant – yeah. 'Are yeh alrigh', Sharon?'

— The head on him. 'Did yeh not see me at the vegetables?'

— It must be hard, though, sometimes. For actors, like.

— Why?

— They become known as the character they play in the fillum or the television thing. I'd say even their fuckin' families forget who they really are.

— Pitfall of the job, I'd say. Or a blessin'.

— He was Pat Mustard as well – in *Father Ted*.

— Well, there yeh go. It's like he played for both Barcelona *and* Real Madrid.

— 'I'm a very careful man, Father.' My gang are devastated – at home. They all grew up with Georgie Burgess an' Pat Mustard. Even the ones tha' weren't born when they came ou'. They're goin' around quotin' all the lines.

— Same with us. Come here – we've one o' the grand-kids stayin' the nigh'. He's only four – a lovely kid, he's fuckin' gas. We're all sittin' around the table – havin' the dinner, like. An' he finishes his last chip an' he gets up. 'Now to ride Mrs O'Reilly,' he says an' he walks out into the hall.